Do you love nature like Lottie? Do you care
for every little thing on our planet?

Then you can help.
Every little thing YOU do matters A LOT!

Samira

Look out for this sticker for
tips on how YOU can help nature!

BY JANE CLARKE   ILLUSTRATED BY JAMES BROWN

LOTTIE
L♥VES NATURE

Bee-ware!

FIVE QUILLS

♡ HI! ♡

My name is Lottie and I love nature!

♡ LOTTIE ♡

When I grow up, I am going to be a wildlife show presenter like Samira Breeze who presents Every Little Thing.

EVERY LITTLE THING MATTERS

People are part of nature. If nature thrives so do we!

I am keeping notes about lots of cool stuff about nature, wildlife and the Earth.

EVERY LITTLE THING MATTERS!

MY PETS

Did you know that a fully-grown macaw can weigh as much as a cat?

Did you know dogs are descended from wolves?

EINSTEIN

NACHO

♡ ≋ NATURE NOTE ≋ ♡

There are hundreds of different types of parrots, including budgerigars. Parrots love to mimic people, and imitate noises. They can live as long as humans.

I live with my mum and my twin brother Al. He hates spiders, but loves Science!

To Joyce and beekeepers everywhere, with thanks! – J.C.

For Jo, with love X – J.B.

LOTTIE LOVES NATURE: BEE-WARE!

First published in Great Britain in 2021 by Five Quills
93 Oakwood Court, London W14 8JZ

www.fivequills.co.uk

Five Quills and associated logos are a trademark of Five Quills Ltd.

Text copyright © Jane Clarke 2021
Illustrations copyright © Five Quills 2021

Edited by Natascha Biebow at Blue Elephant Storyshaping
Designed by Amy Cooper

A CIP record for this title is available from the British Library

ISBN 978 1 912923 08 3

1 3 5 7 9 10 8 6 4 2

Printed and bound in Great Britain by Clays Ltd, Elcograf S.p.A.

MIX
Paper from
responsible sources
FSC
www.fsc.org   FSC® C018072

CONTENTS

Minibeast Jungle

Lottie Boffin gently pushed her parrot off her nature notebook. Nacho flapped up onto her shoulder and nibbled at her ear. Lottie smiled. Ever since she'd inherited the macaw that her Great Aunt Pru had re-homed from a rescue centre, Nacho had decided she was his new best friend.

"It's hard to stick sunflower seeds

to the page when you're trying to scrunch them up," Lottie murmured, scratching Nacho's feathery head. She glanced at the TV. Samira Breeze, her favourite wildlife presenter in the whole wide world, was winding up her show, 'Every Little Thing'.

"Every little thing matters!" Sam was saying. "Do our minibeast survey and see if you can attract more bugs into your garden, especially bees and butterflies! And don't forget to send in your nature notes for a chance to be a wildlife presenter on our annual Wildlife Adventure!"

"I'm busy working on it right now!" Lottie exclaimed. She fizzed with excitement every time she thought of that prize. She loved nature and it was her dream to be a wildlife presenter. She'd already set up the minibeast survey yesterday evening.

She'd found Mum's stash of jam jars and dug little holes for them all over the back garden. It was time to check what had fallen in!

Einstein, the Boffins' dog, was already in the garden. He bounded over to Lottie, wagging his tail. Nacho took off with a squawk. Einstein barked at him.

Woof! Woof! Nacho barked back. He was very good at imitating sounds. Lottie sighed. The Boffins' pets loved to wind one another up. If they carried on, they'd get louder and louder and disturb the neighbours. Mr and Mrs Good lived on one side with their cat, Precious, and

Mr Parfitt on the other with his son Noah. Precious and all the grown-ups liked peace and quiet.

"Shhh!" Lottie told them. She settled Nacho on his favourite perching spot on the fence between the Boffins' and the Parfitts' gardens. Nacho liked it because he could keep an eye on what was happening on both sides. Below it, was an upturned empty flowerpot and a cluster of young sunflower plants that Lottie had planted from seeds she'd picked out of Nacho's parrot food. She couldn't wait to see how many flowers she would have and how tall they would grow.

Einstein followed Lottie round the garden, snuffling into each of the jam jars as, one by one, she unearthed them. "Ooh!" Lottie exclaimed, holding up the jar she had placed near the pond. Inside it, she could see three woodlice curled into tiny balls, a shiny black beetle, a tiny spider and a little centipede. She made a note of what she found, and released the occupants. In the other jars, she found some snails, lots more woodlice, a few ladybirds, beetles and centipedes, and a grasshopper. The garden was a minibeast jungle!

MY MINIBEAST SURVEY

Minibeasts are good for nature!
They're important food
for creatures like frogs,
birds and hedgehogs.

On a dry* evening, I put empty
jam jars in the ground in
different parts of my garden.

(You can also use empty
yoghurt cartons.)

TIP: Make sure the
tops of the jars are
level with the ground.

*If it is rainy, the containers could fill with
water and your minibeasts might drown.

The next day, I collected the jam jars.
Don't forget or your minibeasts might starve!

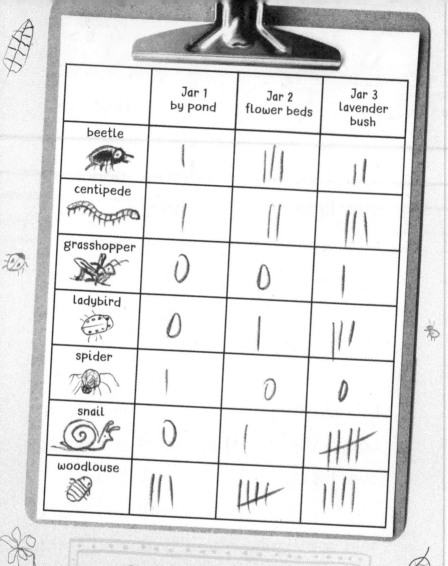

	Jar 1 by pond	Jar 2 flower beds	Jar 3 lavender bush
beetle	I	III	II
centipede	I	II	III
grasshopper	0	0	I
ladybird	0	I	III
spider	I	0	0
snail	0	I	IIIII
woodlouse	III	IIIII	IIII

Remember to recycle the
yoghurt pots and jam jars.

Make sure you release
your minibeast afterwards!

Lottie gently tipped the little brown grasshopper out of the jam jar onto her hand. She quickly cupped both hands around it as the garden gate creaked open.

"Hola!" screeched Nacho as Noah Parfitt came in, clutching a small yellow dumbbell in each hand.

"Your mum is expecting me round this afternoon," he said, peering at Lottie through the hair that flopped over his eyes.

"She is," Lottie confirmed. "She said something about your dad going out to play golf?"

"Correct!" Noah squatted up and down, curling his forearms to his chest.

Lottie tried not to smile. Ten year-old Noah was a very clever computer programmer, but he never remembered to tie his shoelaces properly.

It was Noah's dream to live on Mars. "These are Dad's dumbbells," he explained to Lottie. "He uses them to strengthen his arms to improve his golf swing. But I'm using them to make my muscles strong enough to help build the first settlement on Mars."

Noah looked round the garden. "Where's Al today? Working on his time machine?"

"That's a secret!" Lottie reminded him. They didn't want Mum to find out the reason for her science-mad twin brother's experiments. "Al's at

Mia's house. They're working on a joint Maths project, making a model Eiffel Tower out of matchsticks and mini-marshmallows."

"They'll need a lot!" Noah exclaimed. "Hey! What do you have in your hands?"

Lottie carefully opened her fingers. Noah stepped forward to take a closer look. As his shadow fell over it, the grasshopper sprang away.

"Wow, that jumped a long way," Lottie said.

"It must have really strong legs," Noah agreed. "If my legs were that strong I could do all sorts of amazing things on Mars!"

"But human beings can never jump like that because our legs are different," Lottie said. "We're animals and animals have bones on the inside. Insects' skeletons are on the outside."

"But I could design and wear an exoskeleton!" Noah told her. "Computer programmers and engineers are already working on them to help people who have lost the use of their arms and legs."

Noah looked thoughtful. "If I had a robo-exoskeleton, I wouldn't need

to use Dad's dumbbells to build my muscles after all." He gave the dumbbells one last, big swing. One shot out of his hand, and over the Parfitts' fence, narrowly missing Nacho.

Squawk! Nacho screeched in alarm as he took off.

Woof! Woof! Woof! Einstein barked.

Woof! Nacho echoed, circling above the Parfitts' garden.

"Hey!" yelled Noah's dad. "I'm trying to play golf here!"

Bumbling About

"Sorry, Dad!" Noah called.

Lottie stood on the edge of the flowerpot near the fence so she could look over into the Parfitts' garden. Mr Parfitt had turned it into a mini golf course by covering the entire garden with artificial grass. "There probably won't be any minibeasts living next door at all," Lottie thought, "but if there are any, they'll need rescuing!"

"Hello, Mr Parfitt," Lottie called. "Please can I check to see if any bugs have fallen into your golf holes? I'll re-home any I find," she added quickly.

Mr Parfitt was staring at the dumbbell. It was sticking out of one of his golf holes. His mouth opened and closed, but no sound came out.

"He's just standing there looking stunned!" Lottie called down to Noah. "We'd better check he's okay!"

They hurried round to Noah's house.

"It didn't hit you, did it, Dad?" Noah asked anxiously.

"Noooo." Mr Parfitt slowly picked up the dumbbell and gazed at it in awe. "Hole in one," he muttered. "I've played golf all my life and never got a hole in one, but you did, Noah!"

"I did?" Noah shrugged.

"You don't even appreciate it," Mr Parfitt sighed. He handed the dumbbell to Noah and went inside.

Noah dumped both dumbbells beside the fence close to his back gate and went to help Lottie check the golf holes. There was an ant or two, but most of them were empty.

"There's hardly any wildlife in your garden," Lottie said sadly. "Artificial grass doesn't help nature at all."

"Hey! I found a caterpillar!" Noah called. He was standing next to the hole beneath the apple tree branch that hung over from Lottie's garden.

"It must have dropped in from the branch." Lottie carefully scooped out the caterpillar. It was as long as her little finger, and almost as fat. It was amazing to think it would turn into a butterfly.

Nacho swooped down onto Lottie's shoulder in a flurry of brightly-coloured wings.

Nacho bobbed his head up and down and stared at the caterpillar.

"No, you can't eat it," Lottie told him. Nacho flapped back to his perching place.

"I thought bugs like this caterpillar were important food for birds," Noah laughed.

"Not this bird. He gets plenty of parrot food!" Lottie said. "But you're right — lots of creatures rely on bugs and insects for food."

"They're very nutritious," Noah said. "I expect we'll breed and eat them on Mars!"

Noah's dad came back out, clutching a mug of tea.

"We found a caterpillar!" Lottie said, thrusting it under his nose.

Mr Parfitt took a step back. "Take it away," he told Lottie. "I don't like nasty wriggly, squishy things."

"I think it's fascinating," Lottie said. "And it will turn into a butterfly. Everyone likes those!"

"I don't," Mr Parfitt declared. "Flappy things are even worse than wriggly, squishy things."

Just then, a fat fuzzy bumblebee buzzed past his ear.

Mr Parfitt started in fright and almost dropped his mug. Tea splattered down his front.

"Flappy, buzzy things are the very worst!" he declared. "They can put you right off your golf. Petunia hates them, too."

Mr Parfitt looked at his watch. "That reminds me, I need to change and check my golf equipment before she arrives." He headed back inside.

"Petunia's picking him up later, and they're going to play a round of golf at the Royal Berkley Golf Club," Noah told to Lottie. "It's really posh!"

"Hmmm." Lottie wasn't really listening. She was busy watching the bee bumble around the Parfitts' garden.

"It's looking for a flower," she said, "but it won't find any here. It's such a shame. Bees are really important! They take pollen from plant to plant so they can form fruits and seeds."

IMPORTANT INSECTS

GRASSHOPPER

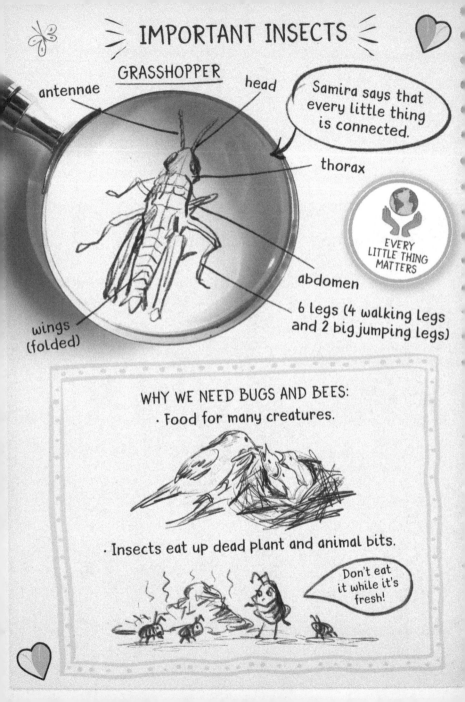

antennae

head

Samira says that every little thing is connected.

thorax

abdomen

EVERY LITTLE THING MATTERS

6 legs (4 walking legs and 2 big jumping legs)

wings (folded)

WHY WE NEED BUGS AND BEES:
- Food for many creatures.

- Insects eat up dead plant and animal bits.

Don't eat it while it's fresh!

Insects are important for pollinating crops and flowers.

Pollen is transferred from the male to the female part of the flower. This fertilizes the plant so it can make fruit and seeds. **Bees** are very important pollinators!

"Computer scientists and engineers are working on tiny swarm robots to help pollinate plants," Noah said. "Imagine having a garden filled with robo-bees!"

Lottie shuddered. "I don't want robo-insects in my garden. I want real ones, like this." She pointed to the bumblebee. It was buzzing around the yellow dumbbells Noah had dropped by the gate. "Your garden is a bit of a disaster for nature. But I'm going to do everything I can to attract more insects to my garden, especially bees!"

Waggle Dance

Lottie and Noah watched as the bumblebee settled on one of the yellow dumbbells. They were so close they could see a cluster of yellow pollen on the hind pair of its hairy legs.

"He seems to like yellow," Noah commented.

"He's a she," Lottie corrected him. "Only female bees have pollen

collectors on their legs.
But you're right, bees
like yellow. That's why
I've planted lots of sunflowers. Maybe
she thinks the dumbbell is a flower."

"This one's not doing any work,"
Noah said. "She's just lying there."

"She looks really tired," Lottie
agreed. She thrust the caterpillar into
Noah's hand. "Hold this. Samira says
you can help revive an exhausted bee."

Lottie dashed back to her kitchen
and grabbed Mum's empty coffee mug.
She splashed in a tiny bit of water and
added a couple of teaspoons of sugar.

Then she grabbed Mum's big jam spoon and headed back to the Parfitts'.

Noah watched as she tipped a few drops of sugar water onto the big spoon and quietly and carefully placed it down next to the bee.

"Shouldn't you leave her the mug-full?" he asked.

"She only needs a tiny bit," Lottie said. "She could drown in a mug. And we're not going to leave the spoon out for long. I have to get it back to Mum."

Noah stared at the bee. "She's very big and fuzzy!" he said.

"She is," agreed Lottie. "Bumblebees

are big, but they live in small nests in the ground so you don't see that many together. You're lucky to have her in your garden. Most of the bees I see buzzing about are little honeybees."

"Honeybees are the ones that live in hives, aren't they?" Noah asked.

"Yes, with thousands of others," Lottie confirmed. "That's another reason for not leaving this sugar spoon out for long. What if a honeybee found it and went back to tell the rest of the hive and thousands of bees turned up?"

"Dad wouldn't like that one bit!" Noah laughed.

"Better not tell him about this one, then," Lottie said. "Let's leave it to find the sugary water and have a rest in the sun. We can go back to my house and re-home the caterpillar."

Noah gently laid the caterpillar under the bush that Lottie chose for it.

"I was thinking about that bee," he said. "How would she tell another bee where the food is? Does she have a special buzz?"

"I don't know how bumblebees do it," Lottie confessed. "But honeybees go back to the hive and do a dance."

"How does that work?" Noah asked curiously.

"Scientists who have studied them say that if food or water is close, they do a circle dance." Lottie circled around flapping her hands like a bee's wings. "That tells them to circle out of the hive to find it."

There was an excited **squawk!** Nacho flew over her head and began to circle with her.

"But if the food source is a long way away, honeybees do a waggle dance." Lottie giggled. She began to move in a figure of eight, flapping her hands and waggling her rear end.

Einstein followed her, waggling his tail, too.

"Very funny," Noah grinned. "But I still don't understand how that tells other bees anything."

"I'll explain if you give it a go," Lottie said.

"Okay!" Noah held his arms close to his chest and flapped his hands.

"You start the dance in the direction of the food. That's it!" Lottie encouraged Noah.

The back gate creaked open. It was Al.

"Come and join our experiment,"

Lottie called. She knew her twin brother could never resist an invitation to experiment. "We're working out how bees do a waggle dance."

"Awesome!" Al flapped his hands

and joined in their figure of eights.

"Waggle your bottoms!" Lottie ordered. "The number of waggles you do tells the other bees how far away the food is," she puffed. "Point your bottom upwards or downwards to show if you have to fly up towards the sun or lower down! You got it! Don't forget to buzz!"

They waggled round the garden, buzzing.

Nacho tried to imitate them, but his buzzing was very squawky.

"This is so silly!" Lottie collapsed in a giggling heap, followed by Noah and

Al. Einstein continued chasing round the garden, wagging his tail so hard it was a blur.

Nacho was still parroting **buzz**, **buzz**, **buzzzzzzzzzz**.

"He's getting quite good at buzzing," Lottie gasped.

Tears of laughter were streaming down Al's face. "I only came back to get some more marshmallows and toothpicks," he spluttered.

The kitchen door opened and Mum came out. "I thought I heard bees," she said, puzzled.

"It's only us," Lottie told her.

"Nice to see you having fun!" Mum smiled. "I'm planning to make some jam from the strawberries that didn't sell in our shop, but I seem to have mislaid my jam spoon. And I can't find the jam jars, or my coffee mug anywhere. Have you seen them?"

"*Erm,*" Lottie coughed. "Here's your coffee mug." She fetched it from where she'd left it – on its side, near the caterpillar's new bushy home. "Sorry, it's a bit sticky and dirty," she apologised.

Mum took the mug. "Thank you. So, what are you up to?" she asked suspiciously.

COOL BEES

There are thousands of species of bees. Some are social and live together, like honeybees and bumblebees, and others live alone, like carpenter and mason bees. Some live in small nests, and some live in hives with thousands of other bees.

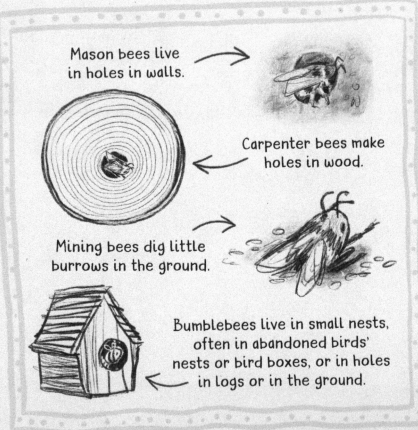

Mason bees live in holes in walls.

Carpenter bees make holes in wood.

Mining bees dig little burrows in the ground.

Bumblebees live in small nests, often in abandoned birds' nests or bird boxes, or in holes in logs or in the ground.

4 wings – Wings can flap 200 times a second.

6 legs
(On worker bees, the two hind legs have pollen baskets.)

5 eyes –
(2 big, compound eyes and 3 light sensors). Bees can see in colour.

🐝 – – – – ⚠️ STINGER ⚠️ – – – 🐝

Honeybees die if they sting you (barbed stings pull out their insides) so they only sting you if they're in danger. Only the females have stings.

OUCH! Bee stings hurt, but they're only dangerous if you are allergic to them.

If something makes a wasp panic (like Nacho flapping his wings at it), it'll release a chemical that calls more wasps to come and help.

Bug-ingham Palace

"I was using your empty jars to collect minibeasts," Lottie explained. "And we found a bumblebee that needed some sugar water to revive it, so I used your jam spoon. I'll get everything back to you later if that's OK? Then I'll help you make the jam."

"I don't need them right now," Mum said. "I'll have to watch the jam while it boils, so we can't begin until after I close the shop." Mum smiled. "Your dad would be proud of you, helping bees. He loved nature as well as science."

"I know. And you help nature too. You have local honey and organic fruit and veg in the shop." Lottie gave her mum a big hug. Her dad had died when she and Al were young so they didn't miss him nearly as much as Mum did. Sometimes Lottie wished Al could really invent a time machine to take their mum back to when she was so happy.

"I'm stocking candles made of beeswax, too," Mum said. "The local beekeeper makes them, as well as bringing in the honey!"

"Maybe we could ask her if we could have a beehive in our garden?" Lottie said hopefully.

The shop bell rang. "I'm sorry, Lottie," Mum said as she hurried off. "Beehives need grown-ups to look after them, and I'm too busy with the shop to help."

"Good try!" said Al.

"Never mind," Lottie said. "We can make a home for solitary bees instead."

"We?" said Al and Noah together.

"Yes, if you both help, we can make a brilliant bug hotel. It can be used by all sorts of bugs as well as bees! We'll need stones and logs and sticks and bits and pieces like dry grass or straw. We can also use bark and pine cones and hollow bamboo canes . . . Al, you look in the garage and see if you can find a bit of cardboard. Preferably the bumpy sort. We'll crumple it up."

"My dad has some bamboo canes that he's cut up to use for his golf flags," Noah said. "I'll fetch some."

Al went off and reappeared with some corrugated cardboard and a couple of old roof tiles. "There are some old bricks in the garage, too," he said. "I'll bring them out."

"Great!" Lottie chose a level spot near the pond and laid the bricks flat, in a square. Then she began to pile the other things on top, making sure that each layer was sturdy and strong before adding the next. Nacho strutted backwards and forwards, bringing pieces of dry grass. Einstein dragged over a large stick that had fallen off the apple tree.

"It doesn't matter where things go as long as we don't make it so high it falls over. We just stack everything up and create lots of little holes," Lottie said, attempting to remove the stick from Einstein's jaws. He ran off to the other end of the garden with it.

Al added the old roof tiles to the top.

Lottie stood back and admired their bug hotel. It was knee-high and in the shape of a house. There were lots of tiny nooks and crannies for bugs and insects to shelter in.

"It's more like a bug palace than a hotel!" Noah laughed.

"It's perfect," Lottie said. "And it's next to the pond, so every little thing can get a drink."

"I'm a big thing, and I need a drink after all that work," Al laughed.

Nacho swooped down onto Lottie's shoulder as they headed for the kitchen. He found a perch on the back of a chair as they stood by the sink and glugged down glasses of water.

"Mia will be wondering where I've got to," Al told them. "It's time I went back to her house. See you later!"

Lottie bent over the sink to rinse out her glass. Something splatted on the floor behind her. "Parrot poop!" she thought, in dismay. She'd hoped she'd trained Nacho not to do that inside.

She bent down to peer at it more closely. It wasn't parrot poop – it was strawberry. Mum had left a bowl of strawberries for the jam on the kitchen table. Nacho had been pinching them and dropping bits on the floor.

Einstein slurped up the strawberry mess.

Noah picked up one of the remaining strawberries. "Yuk!" he exclaimed. "These are ever so squishy."

"Perfect for a butterfly feeder, though." Lottie plopped a handful in her glass and squished them into a mush.

"All we need is something to hang up and smear it on. You can use a paper plate, but we've got plenty of bits of wood. . . " She rummaged in a drawer for a ball of string.

"Come on," she said to Noah. Nacho swooped onto her shoulder.

Outside, Lottie found a short, flat piece of wood left over from one of the wooden crates that they'd used for the bug hotel. Next, she cut off a piece of string that was as long as her outstretched arms. She tied each end of the string around the ends of the plank so it looked like a little swing. Then she smeared the squishy strawberry mixture onto the wood to make the feeder.

Lottie climbed up onto the flowerpot to hang it on an old nail that stuck out of the fence. Nacho hopped off her shoulder onto the fence immediately above the butterfly feeder and started munching.

Einstein stood beneath Nacho, drooling.

"I thought this was a butterfly feeder, not a parrot feeder," Noah murmured.

"Einstein's jealous!" Lottie sighed. "Any minute now," she said, "Nacho will start imitating the woofing. Then the two of them will get louder and louder and the noise will disturb your dad and Mr and Mrs Good. Then they'll all complain to my mum — again!"

Bee-ware!

Lottie and Noah watched as Nacho bobbed his head and stared down at Einstein. Einstein stared back, and gave a polite little **Woof**?

"Here we go," muttered Lottie. But to her surprise, instead of barking back, Nacho took a lump of sugary strawberry and dropped it down to Einstein. Einstein snapped it up and wagged his tail. Lottie watched with a big smile on her face as they did the same again and again – and again.

"It's so good to see Nacho and Einstein becoming friends!" she told Noah.

"They haven't left any fruit for the

butterflies," Noah pointed out.

"Never mind," said Lottie. "There may not be any butterflies, but look, there are loads of bees buzzing around the garden."

"Loads," Noah agreed. "In fact, I've never seen so many in one garden before."

Nacho finished off his strawberry and began to buzzzz along with them.

"These ones are little honeybees!" Lottie exclaimed. "They must like coming here now. Samira says the most important way to help nature in your garden is to create the right habitat."

HABITAT

EVERY LITTLE THING MATTERS

Habitat = a place where living things make their home.

Every little thing needs a place to live!

Samira says lots of animals are threatened because their habitats are being destroyed.

A GOOD HABITAT HAS:

✓ a safe shelter
✓ water
✓ food source nearby

HABITATS IN MY GARDEN:

My pond

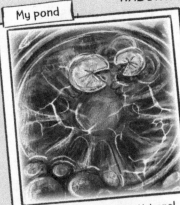

Frogs and bugs like it here!

My bug hotel

Lots of minibeasts live here!

Mum has made a habitat for us in the house.

NACHO

Nacho is a Scarlet Macaw. His natural habitat is the South American Rainforest, but he was rescued as a young fledgling by my Great Aunt Pru.

"We've made the pond and the bug hotel," Lottie went on. "Next year, I'm going to plant even more sunflowers. And maybe some other plants that bugs and bees like, like wildflowers and bushes that flower at different times and produce yummy seeds and berries. That way, there will be food for them all year."

"Making habitats for bugs in your garden is a lot easier than creating homes for humans on Mars!" Noah said. "We'll have to live in pods or domes. But there will be lots of people packed in together, so life will have to be really organised."

"Sounds like living in a beehive," Lottie said. "But I wouldn't want to live in a hive! Each honeybee has a specific role — they can't choose to be anything they like."

"Like a wannabee wildlife presenter like you," Noah joked.

"Or an astronut living on Mars like you!" Lottie countered.

The buzzing noise was becoming louder and louder.

"Nacho's getting better at buzzing," Lottie giggled. "It really sounds like bees!"

NOAH'S NEXT LEVEL:
Living on Mars

In the future, I want to go and live on Mars! Scientists think we can make habitats from Martian rocks using 3D printers.

Our living areas will need to be sealed off from Mars' hostile atmosphere and extreme temperatures. We'll have to wear spacesuits outside.

There is no water, only ice, on Mars. We'll need to collect it and thaw it out.

There's nothing for us to eat on Mars! We can take some food with us, but we will need to grow and produce our own food on Mars.

The average temperature on Mars is -63 °C (-81 °F).

The Earth's average temperature is 15 °C (59 °F).

Only the middle of Antarctica gets as cold as Mars.

Noah stared over her shoulder. His mouth dropped open.

"It isn't Nacho. It really is bees!" Noah pointed at the Boffins' tree.

Lottie whirled round. A cloud of honeybees was clustering on the lowest branch of the Boffins' apple tree overhanging Noah's side.

"They're swarming!" she gasped. "Samira says most swarms happen early in the summer, so it's the right time of year." Lottie stood on the flowerpot to get a better view. It looked as if the branch had grown a big, fuzzy, buzzy beard.

"Is it safe to stay outside?" Noah asked nervously, stepping up on the flowerpot beside her. It was only just big enough for two.

"Samira says it's best to keep your distance from swarms," Lottie said. "We'd better warn your dad."

But before they could take a step in his direction, Mr Parfitt opened the back door and stepped out onto his putting green. He was carrying a golf putter and wearing diamond-patterned trousers and a bright yellow shirt.

"He's come out to practice

his putting," Noah groaned as his dad put down a golf ball, "and he's wearing yellow. What if the bees see him and think he's a flower?"

"What's that buzzing noise?" Mr Parfitt muttered. He picked up the golf ball and put it to his ear, puzzled.

"It's bees!" Noah yelled. Mr Parfitt looked up.

"Turn round and go inside, Dad!" Noah called. But it was no good. Mr Parfitt seemed to be rooted to the spot.

"He's frozen with fear. We'll have to go round and help him," Noah told Lottie. "We can go in through the front door."

"Good idea, we don't want to disturb the swarm," Lottie agreed. They raced next door with Nacho

and Einstein close behind them, and made their way through the house, into the kitchen.

"Sit and stay!" Lottie told Einstein. Nacho perched on the back of a kitchen chair while they quietly opened the kitchen door and slowly tiptoed out into the garden.

The swarm were still buzzing around the branch.

"Dad! Come inside where it's safe!" Noah said, quietly, grabbing his dad's sleeve and tugging.

Mr Parfitt still didn't move.

"Yes, come inside." Lottie took hold of his other sleeve, but he still wouldn't budge.

Woof! Einstein burst out of the kitchen door, grabbed the bottom of Mr Parfitt's trousers and tugged with all his might. Lottie glanced nervously at the swarm, but the bees weren't taking any notice of them.

Beeeees!

There was a loud **rii-iip**.

A big tear appeared in Mr Parfitt's new golfing trousers. Lottie noticed his sock had little green aliens on it. She glanced at Noah.

"Birthday present," Noah confirmed.

"My new trousers!" Mr Parfitt seemed to wake up. "*Bees!*" he shrieked, dashing inside.

Noah, Lottie, and Einstein followed him. Mr Parfitt already had his phone to his ear. "I'm calling an exterminator!" he said. "There's one who lives just round the corner."

"Exterminator!" squawked Nacho.

The front doorbell rang. It was Mrs Boffin.

"I can see the swarm from my kitchen window. Is everything okay?" she asked.

"No!" Lottie cried. "Mr Parfitt is calling an exterminator. It's wrong to kill bees! Call the beekeeper quickly, Mum!"

"Her number's on my phone." Mrs Boffin stepped inside and made the call.

"She's on her way," said Mum. "She'll get here as fast as she can."

The doorbell rang again.

A white van with 'Pest Control' on it was parked on the kerb. A man in a boiler suit with an enormous insecticide spray strapped to his back stood on the front step.

"Mr Parfitt?" the figure said. "Hello. I've come to solve your pest problem."

"Hola!" squawked Nacho.

A Swarm Welcome!

"It's wrong to kill bees!" Lottie told the pest control man. "They're really important!"

The exterminator looked first at her and then at Nacho who was perched on her shoulder.

"Who are you?" he asked. "And what's that dirty great albatross doing on your shoulder?"

"Nacho isn't an albatross. He's a macaw," said Lottie indignantly. "And I'm Lottie. I love nature and bees are an important part of nature."

"Nature can be a pain sometimes," the man grumbled. "I need to speak with the householder. He or she has the right to choose a quick and final solution to any pest problem."

Mr Parfitt stepped forward. "I choose to get rid of the bees," he said. "Now! They have to be gone before Petunia comes to take me to play golf. She hates buzzy things!"

"But insecticide is bad for the planet,"

Lottie said desperately. "And it's really smelly so you won't be able to play golf outside for a couple of days. Plus you'll have lots of dead bees to pick up."

"She's right," Mum and Noah said together.

"Oh." Mr Parfitt looked unsure. Another van drew up and a woman holding a beekeeper's veiled hat and a big box stepped out.

"The beekeeper!" Lottie breathed a sigh of relief. "Let's see what she says."

"Hola!" Nacho greeted her.

"Hola to you. And hello again, Mrs Boffin." The beekeeper smiled.

"I hear there's a swarm of honeybees? I have a new empty hive that will be just the place for them."

"But can you get them all out of here, and quickly?" Mr Parfitt asked. "Without any smells?" he added.

"By nightfall," the beekeeper assured him. "And it won't smell at all. Re-homing a swarm is a simple process if you know what you're doing. All you need is a box with a lid that has a few holes in it for stragglers," the beekeeper continued.

"Oh very well," Mr Parfitt said grudgingly. "If it means I can get back to playing golf quicker, then I choose the beekeeper."

"I'll be off, then." The exterminator stomped back to his van. "I'll send you my call-out bill!"

Lottie breathed a sigh of relief.

"I'll give you my pocket money!" she told Mr Parfitt. "It's worth it to save the bees."

"It is," the beekeeper agreed. "Now, I have a couple of extra hats if anyone wants to watch."

"Yes, please!" said Lottie and Noah.

They each put on a beekeeper hat and tucked the ends of the mesh veils into the necks of their T-shirts. The beekeeper pulled on a pair of gloves that went up to her elbows.

"Do we need gloves, too?" asked Lottie.

"Or boots?" Noah added.

"No," the beekeeper said. "You won't be holding any bees. I'm going to ask you to stand well back."

"Will they sting?" asked Noah.

"A swarm of bees isn't interested in stinging anyone," the beekeeper reassured them. "When they swarm, they have guts full of honey for the new hive, so they're too full to want to sting. But it's better to be safe than sorry. Keep your pets inside," she advised.

"I'll take Nacho and Einstein back home via the front," Mum said.

The others made their way to the back of the house.

"Be as quick as you can, please!" Mr Parfitt said, looking at his watch. "Petunia will be arriving soon. I'd better go inside and freshen up."

Lottie and Noah followed the beekeeper outside. They watched in fascination as she held the open box beneath the swarm and shook the branch they were on. A big blob of buzzy bees plopped in, but some remained on the branch.

The beekeeper placed the box on the ground beneath the branch and put on the lid.

"As long as I've got the queen in the box, the other bees will find her before dark," she explained, giving the tree another shake.

A little honeybee landed on Lottie's veil, right in front of her nose. It stayed there for a second then flew off. Lottie followed it with her eyes until it found the swarm and crawled through one of the small holes into the box.

"That's it for now!" The beekeeper stood patiently until the bees that had landed on her had taken off.

Lottie and Noah followed her to the Parfitts' back door, where they took off their hats and veils.

"Don't disturb the box," the beekeeper told them, gathering up her equipment.

"I'll come back when it gets dark to collect it and tomorrow morning, I'll put them in their new hive as soon as it gets light."

"Thank you! The bees will be happy in a new hive!" Lottie said as they waved her off.

Noah went inside to fetch his dad. Lottie noticed he was still wearing his torn trousers.

"Have the bees all gone? Is it safe to go outside?" Mr Parfitt asked.

"The swarm is in the box. The beekeeper will come back for them when it gets dark," Lottie told him.

"But I wanted them all to be gone before Petunia gets here," Mr Parfitt huffed.

"It's quite safe," Lottie told him. "Come outside and see."

HONEYBEE BEEHIVE HOME

A beehive can hold 50,000 honeybees.
Most are worker bees.

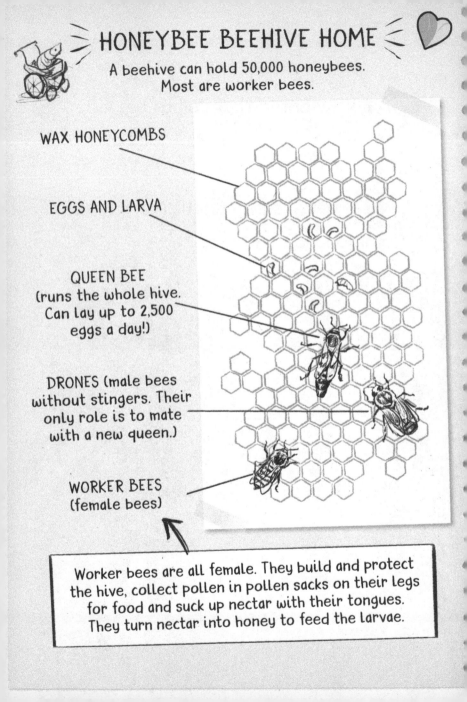

WAX HONEYCOMBS

EGGS AND LARVA

QUEEN BEE
(runs the whole hive.
Can lay up to 2,500
eggs a day!)

DRONES (male bees
without stingers. Their
only role is to mate
with a new queen.)

WORKER BEES
(female bees)

Worker bees are all female. They build and protect
the hive, collect pollen in pollen sacks on their legs
for food and suck up nectar with their tongues.
They turn nectar into honey to feed the larvae.

If the hive gets too crowded, honeybees swarm and leave the hive with a new queen in late spring or early summer.

The honeybee swarm in our apple tree was resting on their journey to find a place to build a new home. The beekeeper had a hive ready for them to move into.

In the wild, honeybees look for a sheltered place, like a hole in a tree trunk, to make their hive.

♡ ≷ COOL FACTS ≶ ♡

All bees make honey for their own (baby) grubs, but only honeybees produce enough for other creatures (like us).

It takes eight honeybees all their lives to make one teaspoon of honey!

(Worker honeybees live around six weeks. Queen honeybees live 2-3 years.)

Lottie, Noah and Mr Parfitt watched as the last bees crawled through the holes to rejoin their swarm.

"Lottie!" Mum's head popped up over the fence. "I need the jam spoon and jam jars now! And what have you done with all the strawberries?!?"

"Uh-oh!" Lottie looked at Noah. "We're on our way back now, Mum," she called. "There's a perfectly natural explanation . . . "

"I'd better return the dumbbells to Dad before we go," Noah picked one up, but the bumblebee was still asleep on the other . . . "

The back gate creaked open, startling them and the bee. Petunia waltzed into the Parfitts' garden.

Lottie and Noah gasped as her foot slipped on the dumbbell.

"WHOOPSIE!" Petunia yelled.

She put out a hand to steady herself on the fence and stop herself from falling.

Lottie winced. There were big blobs of sticky greeny-brown and white parrot poop, right there on the fence.

"Urrgh!" Petunia shrieked, staring at the palm of her hand.

"Petunia my dear! Whatever's the matter?" Mr Parfitt hurried to greet her.

"My hand! **POOP!**" Petunia spluttered, wiping it off on the artificial grass.

Just then, the bumblebee buzzed past Petunia's ear. "**EEEK!** A bee! Get away from me!" she shrieked, backing up against the fence.

"Oh, no!" Lottie murmured. "Now she has parrot poop on her clothes, too!"

"Perhaps she won't notice," whispered Noah.

Petunia was staring at Mr Parfitt. Her eyes widened. "Just look at you! We can't play golf at the Royal Berkley with you looking such a mess. They have a dress code, you know!"

"It's not my fault Einstein tore my trousers!" Mr Parfitt groaned. "And it wasn't Einstein's fault really. He got wound up when Lottie was helping the bees . . . "

"But I was so looking forward to playing at the nice club!" Petunia glared at Lottie. "Why is it always so wild around here?"

Mr Parfitt sighed. "Noah," he said.

"You're the oldest. I had hoped you'd be the sensible one and keep an eye on things."

"I'm sorry! It was my fault," Lottie said. "I was only trying to help nature."

Lottie watched the bumblebee buzz off over the fence into the Boffins' garden.

"Er Petunia . . ." Mr Parfitt sounded concerned. "There's something on your blouse. I think it's parrot poop!"

Petunia whirled round. "Oh no! I'll never get it out!" she shrieked.

"But look! The bee's recovered." Lottie had to raise her voice over Petunia's cries. "Sam says every little thing matters. We did help nature."

"Yep, the bees and bugs are happy, just not the human wildlife."

Noah glanced at his dad who was still trying to console Petunia. "She'll take ages to calm down. I wish I already lived on Mars! Petunia's right. It's wild around here!"

"It is!" Lottie giggled. "Time to escape to my house. You can explain to Mum why there are no strawberries left while I find a quiet place to write up my nature notes. I'm determined to win a place on Samira Breeze's next Wildlife Adventure!"

PLANTS FOR BEES

Samira says you can help bees, butterflies and other pollinators by growing the plants they like.

I'm planning to plant a *wildflower* meadow at the back of our garden.

EVERY LITTLE THING MATTERS

BEES LOVE WILDFLOWERS LIKE THESE:

A lavender bush is great for bees and smells really nice.

If you don't have a garden, Samira says you can grow wildflowers in planter boxes or pots.

Lots of plants to pollinate!

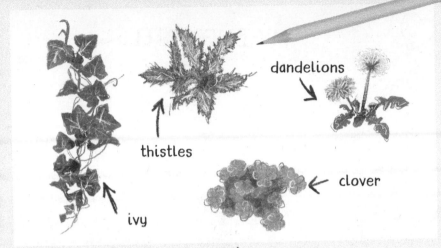

thistles

dandelions

ivy

clover

SUNFLOWERS

GARDEN SEEDS

I'm growing sunflower plants from seeds. The bees will love the bright yellow flowers!

Caterpillars are already nibbling at the leaves.

When they flower, beetles, butterflies and ants will love the nectar as much as the bees do.

 Sunflowers have lots of seeds in the middle. I'm saving some to plant next year.

Yum! Seeds for mice and birds.

Roof made
out of old tiles
(wood works too).

DRY STICKS, LEAVES,
STRAW AND BARK
Beetles, woodlice, ladybirds
and spiders like to live here.

Later, I'll put
soil on the roof
and plant
wildflowers.
Bugs and bees
will like that!

ROLLED-UP CARDBOARD
Insects such as lacewings
shelter here.

BAMBOO
Some solitary bees like
to lay eggs in here.

I used bricks,
stones and logs as a
foundation to build on.

WARNING: Be careful
not to build your bug
hotel too high in case
it all falls down on you!

⇝ MY BUTTERFLY FEEDER ⇜

Butterflies flit about when it's a warm and sunny day.
(They don't like cold, windy and wet weather.)

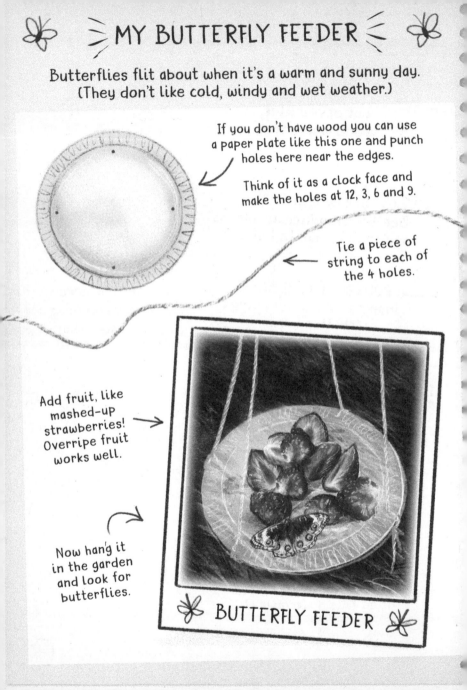

If you don't have wood you can use a paper plate like this one and punch holes here near the edges.

Think of it as a clock face and make the holes at 12, 3, 6 and 9.

Tie a piece of string to each of the 4 holes.

Add fruit, like mashed-up strawberries! Overripe fruit works well.

Now hang it in the garden and look for butterflies.

✿ BUTTERFLY FEEDER ✿

Butterflies like overripe fruit, but so does Nacho!

BUTTERFLY FACTS

· Butterflies and their caterpillars are an important food source for other creatures, like bats and birds.

· Butterfly caterpillars eat plants.

· Most adult butterflies use their long tongues to sip nectar from flowers and fruits.

EVERY LITTLE THING MATTERS

SAMIRA'S CONSERVATION CORNER

Are you helping to protect nature in your garden or neighbourhood, like Lottie? Then you're a conservationist. All over the world, conservationists are working hard to prevent species from becoming extinct.

EVERY LITTLE THING MATTERS

♡ WHAT YOU CAN DO: ♡

Everything in nature is connected so it's important to help save all plants and animals!

Samira

One third of the world's food supply is pollinated by bees. Without bees, people and animals wouldn't have very much to eat. But bees are in danger! The number of bees is declining because of habitat loss, climate change and the use of harmful pesticides.

Bees on honeycomb

Short-haired bumblebee

This is the big, fat short-haired bumblebee. The species was declared extinct in the UK in 2000, so it comes from Sweden. Conservationists created a flowery habitat in Dungeness in Kent, England, and released it and other Swedish bumblebees in the hope that they will set up a new colony there.

IT'S ALWAYS WILD WITH LOTTIE ABOUT!

LOTTIE LOVES NATURE

Frog Frenzy

BY JANE CLARKE   ILLUSTRATED BY JAMES BROWN

Lottie's golf-mad neighbour has filled in the frogs' pond and is ridding his putting green garden of all the ants. Can Lottie rescue all the wildlife in time?

Discover more **Lottie Loves Nature** adventures at:
www.fivequills.co.uk